PUFFIN BOOKS

Sheltie Finds a Friend

Make friends with

The little pony with the big heart

Sheltie is the lovable little Shetland pony with a big personality. He is cheeky, full of fun and has a heart of gold. His best friend and new owner is Emma, and together they have lots of exciting adventures.

Share Sheltie and Emma's adventures in

SHELTIE THE SHETLAND PONY
SHELTIE SAVES THE DAY
SHELTIE AND THE RUNAWAY
SHELTIE TO THE RESCUE
SHELTIE IN DANGER

Peter Clover was born and went to school in London. He was a storyboard artist and illustrator before he began to put words to his pictures. He enjoys painting, travelling, cooking and keeping fit, and lives on the coast in Somerset.

D1392195

Also by Peter Clover in Puffin

The Sheltie series:

Sheltie Finds a Friend

Peter Clover

PUFFIN BOOKS

For Dorothy, Tony,
Sarah, and Miles

PUFFIN BOOKS

Published by the Penguin Group
Penguin Books Ltd, 27 Wrights Lane, London W8 5TZ, England
Penguin Books USA Inc., 375 Hudson Street, New York, New York 10014, USA
Penguin Books Australia Ltd, Ringwood, Victoria, Australia
Penguin Books Canada Ltd, 10 Alcorn Avenue, Toronto, Ontario, Canada M4V 3B2
Penguin Books (NZ) Ltd, 182–190 Wairau Road, Auckland 10, New Zealand

Penguin Books Ltd, Registered Offices: Harmondsworth, Middlesex, England

First published 1996
1 3 5 7 9 10 8 6 4 2

Created by Working Partners Ltd, London W6 0HE

The moral right of the author/illustrator has been asserted

Filmset in 14/20 Palatino

Made and printed in England by Clays Ltd, St Ives plc

Chapter One

It was a lovely spring day in Little Applewood. Emma was in the paddock with Sheltie. They were playing Frisbee. Emma was trying to teach the little Shetland pony to catch the saucer-shaped disc.

Sheltie was a clever pony and enjoyed every minute of this new game. He wasn't very good at it though. He couldn't catch for all the tea in China.

Emma threw the frisbee and watched it sail through the air. The disc landed at Sheltie's feet and the little Shetland pony gave a loud snort. He shook his long shaggy mane.

Sheltie bent his head and picked up the frisbee between his teeth. Then, with a sudden flick, he tossed the plastic saucer up into the air.

Little Joshua was sitting on the paddock fence with Mum, watching the game. He clapped his hands together as Sheltie sent the frisbee spinning over his head.

'Sheltie must be the only pony in the world who can do that,' said Mum.

Emma took a packet of peppermints
from her jacket pocket and gave
Sheltie one of his favourite treats.

'He's not very good at catching
though,' said Emma. But it didn't
matter. Sheltie was a pony, not a
person. And Emma laughed each time

3

he picked up the frisbee and tossed it
backwards over his head.

The very next morning there was a
surprise waiting for Emma down in
the paddock.

Every day, the first thing Emma
did when she woke up was to look at
Sheltie out of her bedroom window.
This morning when Emma looked,
she could hardly believe her eyes.

As usual, Sheltie was standing by
the paddock gate with his fuzzy chin
resting on the top bar of the wooden
fence. But standing there right next to
him was a little black donkey.

Emma rubbed her eyes and looked
again.

'Where did *he* come from?' said

Emma. She pulled on her school uniform and hurried downstairs.

Mum and Dad were already sitting at the breakfast table. They were both wearing huge grins.

'Have you seen the donkey, Emma?' said Dad. 'His name is Mudlark.'

'Who does he belong to?' asked Emma. She couldn't wait to rush out to the paddock for a closer look.

Chapter Two

The little black donkey was almost
the same size as Sheltie. But not quite
so fat.

They stood side by side in the
paddock, looking over the fence and
up into the garden. When the
donkey saw Emma he threw back
his head and brayed with a loud
hee-haw.

Emma laughed and reached over to

stroke Mudlark's furry head. His
mane felt very bristly.

Sheltie gave a snort and nudged
the donkey with his soft muzzle.
Mudlark gave another bray and his
long ears waggled like a big rabbit's.

'Isn't he funny?' said Mum. She
picked Joshua up so that he could see
better.

'Do you remember us telling you
about Marjorie Wallace, Emma?' said
Dad. 'She's the old lady who lives in
the cottage at the foot of Beacon Hill.'

Emma remembered. Marjorie
Wallace had nine cats. She took in
strays and found homes for
unwanted kittens.

'Well, Mudlark belongs to
Marjorie,' said Mum. 'The poor old

lady hasn't had a holiday for ages.
She doesn't like to leave her cats and
never goes anywhere outside the
village.'

'Marjorie has a sister,' said Dad.

'And a brother somewhere,' said
Mum.

'Yes, but nobody knows much
about him,' said Dad. 'Anyway,
Marjorie hasn't seen her sister for six
years. So all her friends in Little
Applewood thought it would be a
good idea if Marjorie went for a visit.
And we're helping out by looking
after Mudlark while she's away.'

Emma thought this was a
wonderful idea. And Sheltie thought
it was fun too. He blew a raspberry
and gave Mudlark a gentle push.

The little donkey brayed, then galloped around the paddock. Sheltie was close at his heels, playing chase.

'Who will be looking after Marjorie's cats?' asked Emma.

'Mrs Marsh is staying at the cottage while Marjorie's away. And the gardener said he would pop in from time to time to make sure everything is all right.

'One of Marjorie's cats has kittens, Emma. We thought you and Sheltie might like to ride over there after school to see them.'

'Oh, yes please,' said Emma.

Joshua started to wriggle in Mum's arms. He wanted to go and see the kittens too.

Emma unlocked the paddock gate and gave Sheltie and Mudlark their breakfast. Dad had put a bucket in Sheltie's field shelter for Mudlark. The bucket was pushed tightly into an old car tyre so that it wouldn't get kicked over.

Emma stood back and watched Sheltie and Mudlark feeding. They both gobbled their breakfast down in seconds.

Next, Emma filled the water trough with the hose. Mudlark blew bubbles in the water. Emma gave him a squirt and Mudlark threw back his head with a loud hee-haw. Sheltie answered with a loud snort and chased him across the paddock.

'I don't know which one is worse,'

laughed Mum. 'Sheltie or Mudlark. I can see you're going to have your hands full this week, Emma!'

Chapter Three

After school, Emma rode Sheltie over to Marjorie Wallace's cottage at Beacon Hill. Emma was looking forward to seeing the kittens.

The cottage nestled at the foot of the hill, which was on the outskirts of the village.

As Sheltie trotted along towards the cottage, Emma saw someone hop over Marjorie's low garden wall.

She had never seen this man
before. He was quite old, dressed in
rough-looking clothes and was
carrying a sack. Emma was too far
away to see him properly, but she
watched as he disappeared into the
woods behind the cottage. Perhaps it
was the gardener, she thought.

Emma dismounted and led Sheltie
through the garden gate and up the
path to the front door.

There was a big metal ring in the
cottage wall. Emma tied Sheltie's rein
to the ring and knocked on the red
painted door.

Emma waited but nobody came.
She knocked again, louder this
time, and heard footsteps inside.
The cottage door swung open and

Mrs Marsh stood on the front step.

'Hello,' said Emma. 'I've come to see the kittens.' She gave Mrs Marsh her biggest smile.

'Oh dear,' said Mrs Marsh. 'You had better come in, Emma. You see, one of the kittens has gone missing. I can't find it anywhere. Perhaps you can help me find it.'

Emma hunted high and low, all over the cottage. She looked in all the places she could think of where a kitten might hide.

She even looked outside, but there was no sign of the kitten anywhere.

'Perhaps it wandered off to explore,' she said. 'It'll come back when it's hungry. Cats always do.'

'But it's so tiny,' said Mrs Marsh. 'I

14

can't think where it could have gone.'

Emma stayed for half an hour and played with the other kittens. But when it was time to leave there was still no sign of the missing one.

As Emma and Sheltie rode away, Emma suddenly remembered the old man with the sack – the man she had seen hop over the garden wall and disappear into the woods.

I wonder what he had in that sack, thought Emma. Perhaps it was the kitten!

*

Back in the paddock, Dad was busy
fitting Mudlark with a special harness.
Emma's eyes grew wide as she
watched Dad wheel a funny little cart
out from behind Sheltie's field shelter.

Sheltie gave a loud snort and
Mudlark answered with an even
louder hee-haw.

'What's that for?' asked Emma. She
jumped out of the saddle to take a
better look.

The little cart was painted in bright
colours, with swirly patterns. It had
two big wheels, and a little seat at the
front. Two long shafts fitted perfectly
into Mudlark's harness. The cart
looked like a small pony trap.

'It's Mudlark's fish cart,' said Dad.
'Before Marjorie adopted Mudlark he

belonged to her brother, who used to sell and deliver fresh fish to the houses in the village. That was years ago, before her brother went off, but Marjorie still uses the cart to collect her weekly shopping. Mudlark loves to pull it along and give rides, don't you, Mudlark?'

The little black donkey replied with a loud hee-haw.

'Would you like a ride, Emma?' said Dad.

'Oh, yes please,' said Emma. But first she took Sheltie's saddle off and slipped the bridle over his head. She lay them carefully over the top bar of the fence, then climbed into the cart.

Mum came out of the cottage with Joshua, to watch.

Emma took Mudlark's long reins and Dad led the donkey around the paddock. Sheltie thought this was great fun and trotted alongside. He tossed his head and swatted Emma with his swishing tail.

Once Emma was used to the reins, Dad let go and Emma drove the little fish cart around the paddock on her own, in a big circle.

Then Joshua wanted a ride. So Mum lifted him on to the seat next to Emma and Mudlark pulled them both along. Joshua gurgled with laughter as the little cart trundled around the paddock.

When the ride was over, Mum took Joshua inside and put a pizza in the oven for their tea.

Dad took Mudlark out of the
harness and wheeled the cart back
behind Sheltie's field shelter. Then he
went into the cottage to help Mum.

Chapter Four

Emma stayed in the paddock for a
while with Sheltie. She was about to put
his saddle and bridle away when she
noticed a man standing by the fence
talking to Mudlark. The man was
scratching Mudlark's ears and the
donkey was enjoying every minute of it.

The man looked like the old
gardener that Emma had seen earlier
at Marjorie's cottage.

'Good afternoon, miss,' said the man politely. 'That's a fine donkey you have there. I could use a donkey like that.'

Emma thought that was a funny thing to say. She pulled a face and said, 'He doesn't belong to us. We're only looking after him for Marjorie Wallace while she's away.'

'Oh,' said the man with a smile. Then he touched his cap politely and said goodbye.

Emma watched the man walk away up the lane. Although she had never seen him before, Emma thought that the man looked very familiar. He reminded her of someone, but she couldn't think who.

Emma quickly put Sheltie's tack away, then rushed inside to tell Mum and Dad.

'It doesn't sound like Mr Rudd, the gardener,' said Dad. 'Perhaps it was the new hired help at Mr Brown's place. He has a workman doing some odd jobs around the farm.'

'Well, I didn't like him,' said
Emma. 'He wanted Mudlark.'

'He was probably just being
friendly,' said Mum.

Dad put some pizza slices on to
plates and Mum carried them to the
kitchen table. They all sat down to eat.

Later that evening, when Emma went
up to bed, she lay awake thinking
about the missing kitten. Emma
wondered if Mrs Marsh had found it
yet. She decided to ride over again
first thing in the morning and find
out.

But the next morning Emma made
a terrible discovery. When she went
to the paddock Mudlark was
nowhere to be seen.

The paddock gate was locked and bolted and there were no breaks in the fence or any holes where the donkey could have escaped. But Mudlark had gone. Emma ran back inside to fetch Mum. Mum could hardly believe it. She went outside to see for herself.

Sheltie was tossing his head and dashing around the paddock.

'Do you know what happened, Sheltie?' said Mum. 'Where's Mudlark gone?'

Sheltie stared up into the branches of an overhanging tree. He gave a loud snort and scraped at the grass with his hoof.

Emma glanced up into the tree and saw a man's flat cap hanging from one of the branches.

'How did that get up there?' said
Emma.

Mum went to fetch a broom. Then
she reached up into the tree and
knocked the cap off the branch.

When the cap fell to the ground
Sheltie rushed over and picked it up
between his teeth. Then with a quick
flick, he tossed it up into the air, just
like a frisbee.

'Did you throw it up there before, Sheltie?' said Mum.

'I think he must have,' said Emma. 'I bet whoever's taken Mudlark dropped it, and Sheltie tossed it up into the tree.'

'We'd better tell Dad and call the police,' said Mum.

Chapter Five

Half an hour later PC Green arrived
on his bicycle. He examined the
padlock and chain, and the bolt on the
paddock gate, then scratched his head.

'And you say there's no trace of the
donkey anywhere?'

Dad shook his head. 'We've looked
everywhere,'

'And called him,' said Mum. 'He's
definitely gone.'

'Stolen,' said Emma. 'Someone's stolen him! I bet it was that man.'

'We can't be sure of that yet, Emma,' said the policeman.

He looked around the paddock again, checking the fence. But there were no clues to Mudlark's disappearance. Then Mum handed over the cap.

'We found this,' she said. It was an ordinary brown checked cap.

'This could belong to anyone,' said the policeman.

'I bet it belongs to the thief,' said Emma.

'I shall report the incident and organize a search,' said the policeman. 'But I expect, if your donkey *has* been stolen, then he's miles away by now.'

'Oh dear,' said Mum. 'Whatever shall we tell poor Marjorie!'

PC Green looked out in the lane for fresh tyre tracks. But there were none. The weather had been fine for weeks, and the lane was dry and dusty.

There were no footprints either. No hoof marks. No tyre tracks. No clues at all. And no Mudlark.

'Sheltie must have seen who took Mudlark,' said Emma.

PC Green smiled. 'But I'm afraid Sheltie can't tell us, can he, Emma?'

I bet he can, thought Emma. But she didn't say so.

When the policeman left to organize a search, Emma took another look around the paddock.

Mum and Dad went back inside

the cottage. Mum looked very worried. Dad thought it was best not to telephone Marjorie just yet. He didn't want to spoil her holiday. He said they should wait a while and see if the police found Mudlark.

Out in the paddock, Sheltie was nosing about in the long grass by the gatepost. He pawed at the earth and kept pushing his muzzle into a clump of nettles which grew there.

Emma went over to see what Sheltie was so interested in.

Sheltie pushed his head forward into the long grass and gave a loud sneeze. Emma carefully parted the nettles. She found a tiny scrap of red woollen cloth caught on a bramble by the gatepost.

The scrap was no bigger than a postage stamp. Emma took the bit of wool in to show Mum and Dad.

'It could be a piece of jumper or a scarf,' said Mum. 'But none of us has anything that colour. It's probably been there for ages, Emma.'

But Emma didn't think so. She was certain that Sheltie didn't either. They both thought it was a clue.

Emma put the red woolly scrap into her back pocket.

'I hope the policemen find Mudlark soon,' said Emma. 'What would the thieves do with him?'

'Well, he could end up anywhere,' said Dad. 'Probably in a market somewhere, to be sold as a working donkey.'

'Oh, poor Mudlark,' said Emma. 'How awful. He's far too old to work. And he'll miss Marjorie.' She was close to tears. And she kept thinking how horrible it would be if Sheltie had been stolen.

Chapter Six

When Dad came home from work, everyone was sitting around the kitchen table. Emma and Joshua were drawing. All day at school Emma had thought about poor Mudlark. So far she had drawn eight pictures. They were all of donkeys.

Dad telephoned the police station. They told him that their search had found nothing. They had even been

over to Mr Brown's farm to question
the new workman. But the workman
had finished all the odd jobs around
the place. He had even mended the
old rusty lock on the cowshed. Mr
Brown had paid him his wages and
he had already gone on his way.

After tea, Emma decided to ride
Sheltie over to Beacon Hill to visit Mrs
Marsh again. She was hoping that the
kitten had turned up. But there was no
such luck.

'I've been searching and searching,'
said Mrs Marsh. 'And I still can't find
it. It's disappeared.'

'Or been stolen,' said Emma. She
told Mrs Marsh about Mudlark and
the man she had seen hopping over

the garden wall the previous day.

'It couldn't have been Mr Rudd, the gardener. He's not due until tomorrow,' said Mrs Marsh. They both looked puzzled.

'I bet it was that man then,' said Emma. 'And I bet he's taken Mudlark *and* the kitten.'

Mrs Marsh didn't know what to think.

When Emma had to leave, she climbed into Sheltie's saddle and squeezed with her heels.

'Trot on, Sheltie. Trot on.' And Sheltie trotted off. But he wouldn't go the way Emma wanted him to.

Sheltie turned around and went up the path towards the woods behind Marjorie's cottage.

Emma let Sheltie take the lead. They trotted along the path and into the woods.

Emma knew that Sheltie wanted to show her something. He kept his head high and sniffed at the wind as he went along.

A little way into the woods they came to a clearing. Up ahead, sheltered by some overhanging trees, Emma saw a funny-looking caravan.

The caravan was tiny. It looked like a little garden shed on wheels.

Near by, tied to a tree, were two donkeys. One donkey was grey and the other one was almost pure white. It looked like a ghost.

Sheltie sniffed at the air and both his ears pricked up.

Emma slipped out of the saddle.
She and Sheltie were hidden from
view by a thicket of shrubs. They
kept very quiet and watched as an
old man came out of the caravan.

It was the same man that Emma
had seen hopping over Marjorie's
garden wall. And the same man who

had spoken to her in the paddock.
Emma was certain of it.

He did remind her of someone. But
Emma *still* couldn't think who.

She held her breath and watched as
the man untied the white donkey and
led it away, off into the woods.

When he had gone, Emma crept
out from her hiding place. Sheltie
gave a snort and watched her tiptoe
towards the caravan.

Behind the caravan, Emma found a
washing line strung out across two
poles.

On the line was a shirt, a vest and
a pair of red socks. Emma stared at
the socks. Her eyes grew wide and
her heart thumped in her chest.

The socks were the same colour as

the scrap of woolly material that
Sheltie had found by the paddock
gate.

Emma took a closer look at the
socks. And there, in one of them, was
a tear. A hole no bigger than a
postage stamp.

Emma took the woolly scrap out of
her pocket and held it up against the
sock. The colour matched perfectly.
That meant that the man who owned

the socks had been in the paddock.
And he must have stolen Mudlark!

As Emma stood by the caravan she
thought she heard a cat miaow. Emma
listened carefully and pressed her ear
against the painted wood. She heard
the miaow again. The sound was
coming from inside the caravan.

Suddenly, a twig snapped in the
woods. Emma jumped. The man was
coming back. Sheltie gave a warning
blow and Emma ran back and jumped
into the saddle.

She squeezed her heels and Sheltie
took off, trotting back through the
woods and along the path to Beacon
Hill.

Chapter Seven

Emma decided to ride straight back home and tell Mum and Dad what she had discovered.

When she burst in through the kitchen door, Emma was red in the face and out of breath.

She told Mum and Dad all about the funny little caravan in the woods, the socks on the washing line and the cat crying.

When she had finished, Dad reached for the telephone to call PC Green at the station again.

The policeman went to the woods behind Beacon Hill straight away. But when he got there the caravan had gone. There was no sign of it anywhere. No Mudlark and no tracks on the leafy forest floor.

Everyone was very disappointed.

'Perhaps we should telephone Marjorie at her sister's and tell her what's happening,' said Mum.

PC Green thought they should wait a little while longer. The next day was Saturday and there would be three markets in neighbouring villages. Maybe Mudlark would be put up for sale at one of them. PC

Green suggested waiting to see what happened.

'There's no point in causing unnecessary worry,' he said. They all agreed.

'The markets start early in the morning, so we should know by midday if the thief is going to try to sell the little donkey.'

That night, when she went to bed, Emma lay awake thinking about poor Mudlark. She wondered where he was and kept thinking how sad and frightened he must be and how awful it would be for Marjorie when she found out that her donkey had been stolen.

When Emma finally went off to

sleep she had a bad dream. She dreamed that Sheltie had been stolen and she was running all over Little Applewood looking for him. But she couldn't find him anywhere.

In the morning, Emma woke suddenly and jumped out of bed. She ran over to look out of her bedroom window and breathed a sigh of relief. Sheltie was out there in the paddock as usual, looking over the wooden fence.

Everyone was very quiet during breakfast. Emma wasn't hungry at all and pushed her cereal around in the bowl with her spoon.

All they could do was wait and see if Mudlark turned up at any of the markets.

Chapter Eight

At twelve o'clock, PC Green came to the cottage. There was still no news of Mudlark. He hadn't been spotted at any one of the three markets.

'I'm afraid there's not much hope of finding him now,' said the policeman. 'Perhaps you should contact Mrs Wallace after all.'

Mum tried to telephone Marjorie, but there was no reply.

'They must have gone out,' she said. 'I'll try again later.'

Emma thought she would take Sheltie out for a ride over to Beacon Hill again. She wanted to call in on Mrs Marsh to see if the missing kitten had found its way home. Emma kept thinking about the miaowing she had heard from inside the caravan. She was almost certain that it was the kitten.

Emma talked to Sheltie as she plopped the saddle on to his back.

'Do you know where Mudlark is, Sheltie?'

Sheltie tilted his head to one side, listening.

As Emma strapped the leather girth under his fat tummy, she said, 'I bet if anyone can find Mudlark, you can.'

By the time she had fitted the bridle and sat up in the saddle holding the reins, Sheltie was eager to set off.

Emma rode Sheltie out of the paddock and squeezed her heels to send him trotting down the lane.

But Sheltie didn't want to go that way and headed off in the opposite direction. Emma let the reins go slack and Sheltie took the lead.

'Are we going to find Mudlark, Sheltie?' asked Emma. Sheltie blew from his nostrils and quickened his pace.

They crossed Mr Brown's meadow, and rode past Horseshoe Pond to the

back field. There Bramble Woods
began and swept back in a wide arc
all the way across to Beacon Hill. The
woods were much thicker at that end,
and led off, up and over the hills, on
to the open downs and beyond.

Sheltie carried on, following the
bridle path into the woods. They both
knew that track very well. Emma
knew that the thickest part of the
wood lay up ahead.

As they climbed the rise, Emma
looked back and saw Mr Brown's
farm nestling in the fields below. It
was the perfect spot for looking out
across the countryside and the whole
of Little Applewood.

As they reached the top the trees
grew thicker and the ground levelled

out. Sheltie left the track and headed
into the deepest part of the wood.

They hadn't gone far when Emma
gasped. Up ahead, nestling beneath
the trees, was the little caravan. Two
donkeys were harnessed to the
caravan's shafts. The grey one and

the ghostly white one.

Sheltie stopped and Emma slid out of the saddle. Sheltie let out an excited snort. 'Shh,' whispered Emma. She pressed a finger to her lips.

They hid behind a big bush and watched. There was no sign of anyone.

Then Emma heard someone whistling and she saw the old man stepping out of the caravan. He was walking straight towards them. Emma held her breath and whispered to Sheltie to keep still.

Chapter Nine

The man walked straight past them, just ten metres away. He carried on whistling and followed the track down the hill through the woods. He was carrying an empty plastic container. Emma guessed that he was heading for the stream to fetch some water.

Emma and Sheltie watched the man disappear through the trees.

When it was safe to come out of hiding, Emma left the bush and approached the caravan. Sheltie gave a snort and followed.

As soon as the ghostly white donkey saw Emma and Sheltie it threw back its head with a loud hee-haw, just like Mudlark.

Sheltie rushed over and nuzzled the white donkey with his nose as though he were greeting a long-lost friend. The donkey's long ears stood straight up and Sheltie began licking them.

Emma watched as the donkey's ears turned from white to black. Suddenly Emma realized that it *was* Mudlark. He had been covered from head to hoof with white flour!

Emma looked around and wondered
what to do next. Then she heard a
miaow. It's the kitten, she thought.

The sound was coming from inside
the caravan. Emma reached for the
caravan door and gave the handle a
turn. The little door swung open and
Emma stepped inside.

The caravan was very small and

very untidy. There were clothes thrown everywhere, a jumble of old newspapers, and things packed in cardboard boxes. Emma saw a brown checked jacket scrunched up in a ball on the low bunk bed. It was the same colour and pattern as the cap which Sheltie had tossed into the tree.

Curled up in the middle of the jacket was an old grey tabby cat. Not the missing kitten after all. The cat opened one lazy green eye and miaowed.

Outside, Sheltie was becoming very agitated. He gave a snort and scraped at the ground with his hoof. He was shaking his head and blowing loudly.

The man was coming back. Emma

peered through the only window at the rear of the caravan and saw him walking back up the track.

It was too late to run. The man would see her. Clever Sheltie had gone deeper into the woods and was standing behind a clump of bushes. Emma pulled the caravan door closed and stayed inside. She quickly looked around for somewhere to hide.

Suddenly, she noticed a space under the bed and crawled into it.

The caravan door opened and the old man stepped inside. He sat down on the bunk and the bed springs groaned, centimetres above Emma's head.

Emma could see the man's feet and legs in front of her. He was wearing

the red socks, the ones with the hole
in them. Emma could see the hole
quite clearly. It was just above his
shoe. Her heart beat faster and faster.

Chapter Ten

A few minutes passed by. It seemed like hours. The man was talking to the cat, which was purring loudly.

'What a pity we missed Marji, Tigger! Never mind. Maybe we'll see her next time we're passing through. I hope Marji doesn't mind too much about Mudlark. I felt mean taking him like that, but those nice people would never have just handed him over.'

Then the man got up and went outside. He locked the door behind him and Emma heard him climb up into the driving seat at the front of the caravan.

She heard a jangling of reins and the man called out 'Giddy-up!' The caravan rolled forward slowly and bumped across the uneven ground, with Emma inside.

Emma crawled out from under the bed. She peered out of the window and saw Sheltie peeping from behind the thicket, watching as the caravan pulled away.

The caravan was heading up to the open downs and would cross the moor to join the main road.

Sheltie gave a snort and flicked his

tail. Emma didn't know what to do.
She looked at Sheltie and waved her
hands. Get help, Sheltie, she thought.
Go and fetch help. And Sheltie
turned and galloped away, just as
though he had understood.

Sheltie was a very clever pony. He
knew that Emma was in trouble. He

wanted to follow the caravan, but it might be better to bring help.

Sheltie galloped as fast as he could, crashing through the woods along the bridle path back down to Little Applewood.

Sheltie knew the path very well. Every dip and turn. His little legs covered the distance quickly.

Sheltie headed for home. He crossed Mr Brown's meadow and was soon galloping up the lane to the cottage.

Mum and Dad were in the kitchen with Joshua, talking about Marjorie and poor Mudlark. They still hadn't been able to reach her by telephone.

Sheltie came trotting in through the open kitchen door. His hooves clattered on the polished floor tiles.

Mum jumped up out of her chair
with a fright. Joshua giggled as Dad
caught hold of Sheltie's reins.

'Whoa, Sheltie,' said Dad. 'Where's
Emma?'

Mum took Sheltie outside to see if
Emma was in the paddock. Sometimes
Sheltie slipped away from Emma just

for fun. Dad came outside with Joshua. They saw that Emma was nowhere around. Dad called her.

'Emma! Emma!'

There was no reply.

'Something must have happened,' said Mum.

'Emma told me she was going over to visit Mrs Marsh. I'll give her a ring.' Mum hurried inside and picked up the telephone.

Mrs Marsh said she hadn't seen Emma all day. But she told Mum that she would walk the footpath to the top of Beacon Hill and look for her. You could see for miles up there.

Outside, Sheltie was getting impatient. He stamped the ground with his feet and shook his mane.

Then he ran off a little way towards
the paddock and stopped, looking
back at Mum and Dad standing
outside the cottage.

'He wants us to follow him,' said
Mum.

Sheltie trotted into the paddock
and disappeared behind his field
shelter. When Mum and Dad got
there, Sheltie was standing between

the shafts of Mudlark's little fish cart.
He was blowing and snorting like
mad.

'I think he wants you to go with
him in the cart,' said Mum. They
both knew that Sheltie was trying to
help.

Chapter Eleven

Dad quickly slipped Mudlark's special harness over Sheltie and fitted the shafts of the fish cart in place.

'Let Sheltie take you to Emma,' said Mum. 'I'll stay here with Joshua and telephone the police.'

'But how will you know where we are heading?' said Dad.

'I'll watch and see which way you go,' said Mum.

Dad jumped into the fish cart and Sheltie was off. Mum watched as Sheltie pulled the cart out of the paddock, down the lane and across Mr Brown's meadow, heading for the back field and Bramble Woods.

Sheltie was only a little Shetland pony but he was very strong for his size. He pulled the fish cart all the way up the rise where the trees grew thicker and the ground levelled out.

Sheltie didn't stop once. He pulled the cart along the track through the woods and out on to the edge of the downs.

A high ridge swept around and across to Beacon Hill. Mrs Marsh was up there looking for Emma. She stood by the side of the track as

Sheltie trotted up with Dad in the cart.

Mrs Marsh looked surprised.

'Any sign of Emma?' asked Dad.

'I'm afraid not,' said Mrs Marsh. 'But I saw a funny little caravan a moment ago, crossing the clearing over there.' She pointed towards a low rolling slope a short distance away.

'Two donkeys pulling a little caravan,' she said. 'Only minutes ago. It must be heading for the main road.'

The little fish cart flew along. Sheltie galloped as fast as his legs could carry him. The cart bumped down the rolling slope and on to the downs.

Up ahead, they could see the
caravan and the grey tarmac road
beyond. As they drew nearer Dad
suddenly saw Emma peering out
through the caravan window. He was
so surprised that he stood up . . . and
fell out of the cart. He landed on the
grass with a bump, but he was
unhurt.

Sheltie looked back, but he didn't

stop. He could go faster now without Dad's weight in the cart, so he galloped on and soon he was level with the caravan.

The driver was very surprised to see a Shetland pony appear out of nowhere. And even more surprised when Sheltie overtook the two donkeys and stopped suddenly in front of the moving caravan.

The donkeys stopped dead in their tracks and the caravan came to a sudden halt.

The old man jangled the reins and yelled, 'Giddy-up, Mudlark, Sophie.' But the donkeys didn't move. Instead, Mudlark just threw back his head and gave a loud hee-haw!

Chapter Twelve

Everything seemed to happen at once.
A police car came roaring down the
main road. Mum had told the police
that Sheltie was heading in that
direction. The police car screeched to a
halt when the caravan had been
spotted. PC Green jumped out.

Dad was also on his feet and ran
up alongside. He pulled open the
caravan door and Emma stepped out.

The man just sat there holding the limp reins.

'Where on earth did *she* come from?' He could hardly believe his own eyes. He suddenly looked very worried.

Emma ran into Dad's arms.

'I think you've got some explaining to do,' said PC Green.

'Oh dear,' said the man. 'I never meant any harm. I had no idea that the little girl was inside.' The old man was very confused.

'It's true,' said Emma. 'He didn't know I was in there.' Emma thought the man looked very sad. And close up he had a kind face.

Emma suddenly knew who he reminded her of. He looked just like Marjorie Wallace.

Sheltie began to give Mudlark a bath. He was licking the little donkey all over. And the more he cleaned the white donkey, the more the real black donkey showed through.

'A clever trick, covering the donkey in flour,' said PC Green. 'But you didn't fool Sheltie.'

Sheltie gave a loud snort when he heard his name.

'I'm going to arrest you for stealing this animal,' said the policeman. 'Have you anything to say for yourself?'

The old man looked ashamed and lowered his head.

'I'm very sorry,' he said. 'But I didn't really steal him. I was just taking him back.'

'Taking him back? What do you
mean?' asked Dad.

The old man said he was Todd
Wallace, Marjorie's brother.

So that's why he looks so much
like Marjorie, thought Emma.

Todd explained how, years ago, he

74

used to sell and deliver fresh fish to the villagers in Little Applewood.

'Mudlark and Sophie are brother and sister too,' he said. 'I used Mudlark to pull that very same fish cart through the streets.

'When I went off on my travels I left Mudlark behind with Marji. He was too frisky for a caravan and I couldn't look after two donkeys. And Marji did say that I could have Mudlark back whenever I wanted. She always knew I would come back for him one day.'

'But that was a long time ago,' said PC Green. 'And why didn't you tell Marjorie you were coming back for him and just *ask* instead of taking the donkey like that?'

Todd said that Marjorie was bossy and always trying to make him give up his life on the road.

'She wants me to settle down and live in a proper house,' he said. 'I had come to ask, but when I found out that Marji was away, I thought it would be much easier just to take Mudlark and explain later.' He looked at Emma and then at Dad.

'I know that it was wrong to take Mudlark from your paddock,' said Todd. 'But I only wanted Sophie to have some company in her old age. And a little help to pull the caravan.' He looked really sad.

'Well, what you say may be true, but you'll have to stay at the police station until Marjorie gets back and

76

we clear up this mess,' said the
policeman.

'One thing still bothers me though,'
said Emma. 'If you weren't stealing
Mudlark, why did you try to disguise
him by covering him in flour?'

Todd lowered his head.

'I knew everyone would be looking
for Mudlark. And I thought that if I
disguised him then I could get away
quietly without any fuss. I'm very
sorry for all the trouble I've caused. I
really am.'

PC Green drove Todd away in the
back of the police car.

Chapter Thirteen

Dad said he would look after the caravan, Sophie and Tigger the cat. He climbed up into the driver's seat and took the reins. Slowly he turned Mudlark and Sophie around. Then he drove the caravan back up the slope to the top of the rise.

Emma followed behind in the fish cart, with Sheltie pulling it. Sheltie liked the little cart, and Emma thought it was fantastic, steering with the long reins.

They met Mrs Marsh on the crest of the hill. She seemed quite surprised to see Dad driving the caravan, with Emma and Sheltie following behind in the painted fish cart. She gave them a friendly wave and a big smile as they passed.

When they crossed Mr Brown's meadow and drove up the lane, little Joshua could hardly believe his eyes. He was waiting with Mum at the front gate, staring wide-eyed with amazement.

Once safely in the paddock, Dad freed Mudlark and Sophie from the caravan shafts.

Emma unharnessed Sheltie from

the fish cart, then went inside to fetch
a bucket of warm water from the
kitchen.

She got busy with soap and a soft
brush, and soon Mudlark was back to
his normal colour, as black as coal.

Sheltie galloped around the paddock,

chasing Sophie and Mudlark in a game of tag. Mum went inside for some carrots and apples.

'What's going to happen to Mr Wallace?' asked Emma. 'Will he go to prison? And who will look after Sophie?'

'I shouldn't think he will go to prison, seeing that he's Marjorie's brother, Emma. He seemed a nice old man really. And if what he said about Mudlark is true, then I suppose he didn't really steal the donkey anyway. But it was a silly thing to do. We'll have to wait until Marjorie gets back and see what she has to say. In the mean time, there's plenty of room in the paddock. That is, if Sheltie doesn't mind!'

Sheltie shook his mane and let
out a long blow. He didn't mind at
all.

A few days later, Marjorie came back
from her holiday. Emma's dad picked
her up from the train station and
drove her home in the car.

When he sat Marjorie down and
told her all the news, she could
hardly believe her ears.

'Who would have thought that old
Todd would turn up like that!' she
said. 'I often think of him and
wonder what he's up to, travelling
around in that funny caravan all the
time. He never did like living in one
place in a proper house, like the rest
of us. And he carries all his precious

papers and things around in a silly old sack so he doesn't lose them.'

Marjorie was very worried about her brother being held at the police station. She asked Dad if he would drive her there straight away. She wanted to clear up this mess as quickly as possible.

Chapter Fourteen

That afternoon, Marjorie telephoned the cottage and asked if Emma and Sheltie would ride over after school. She said that she had some good news.

When Emma and Sheltie arrived, Marjorie was sitting out in the garden with her nine cats. She was very pleased to see Emma.

'You are such a clever girl, Emma,'

she said. 'And Sheltie is such a clever pony.'

Marjorie had been told all about Emma and Sheltie's adventure and how they had tracked down and found Mudlark.

'It was Sheltie really,' said Emma. 'He found all the clues – the cap and the piece of sock – and he led me to the caravan and Mudlark.'

'Oh yes, I mustn't forget,' said Marjorie, 'I've got a special present for Sheltie.' She went inside and came back with a beautiful leather saddle. It shone like a chestnut.

'This saddle used to belong to Mudlark. But nobody rides him any more. Todd gave me the saddle along with Mudlark and the little painted fish cart over ten years ago when he left. I think it will be just right for Sheltie. It was Todd's idea.'

'Oh, thank you. It's lovely,' said Emma. 'I'll keep it for Sunday best. It can be Sheltie's Sunday saddle.'

Sheltie sniffed at the leather and

blew a loud raspberry of approval.
He liked the Sunday saddle very
much. Emma and Marjorie laughed.
Sheltie could be so funny at times.

'What will happen to your brother?'
asked Emma. 'And Sophie?'

Marjorie gave a big sigh.

'I'm afraid Todd is getting far too
old to go off on his travels any more.
I've sorted everything out with the
police. And I've told Todd that
Mudlark's and Sophie's caravan-
pulling days are over, and that he's
got to settle down.'

'Will he come and live here in
Little Applewood?' asked Emma.

Sheltie pricked up his ears.

'I hope so,' said Marjorie. 'Or one
of the nearby villages.'

'And will he take Mudlark?'

'That's the good news, Emma. Todd said I can have Mudlark for keeps. And Sophie too. I told Todd he will be able to come and visit them whenever he wants. But I hope he decides to come and live here with me. And I hope you and Sheltie will come and visit too, Emma.'

Sheltie pushed his muzzle into Marjorie's hand and blew hot air up her sleeve.

'That would be lovely,' laughed Emma.

'And we've found the missing kitten too,' said Marjorie. 'He'd gone and got himself locked inside the tool shed.'

Everything had turned out fine after all.

Mudlark and Sophie were in their little field behind Marjorie's cottage. Sheltie trotted over on his own and rubbed noses with the two donkeys.

'You're very lucky to have such a clever pony, Emma,' said Marjorie.

'I know,' said Emma. 'Sheltie's the best pony in the world.'